TITANIC

The Story of a Disaster

Dee Phillips

READZONE

READZONE

First published in this edition 2013

ReadZone Books Limited
50 Godfrey Avenue
Twickenham
TW2 7PF
UK

The right of the Author to be identified as the Author of this work has been asserted by the Author in accordance with the Copyright, Designs and Patents Act 1988

Every attempt has been made by the Publisher to secure appropriate permissions for material reproduced in this book. If there has been any oversight we will be happy to rectify the situation in future editions or reprints. Written submissions should be made to the Publishers.

British Library Cataloguing in Publication Data (CIP) is available for this title.

ISBN 978-1-78322-010-6

Printed in China

Developed and Created by Ruby Tuesday Books Ltd
Project Director – Ruth Owen
Designer – Elaine Wilkinson

Images courtesy of public domain, Shutterstock and Superstock (pages 41, 43).

Acknowledgements
With thanks to Lorraine Petersen, Chief Executive of NASEN, for her help in the development and creation of these books

Visit our website: www.readzonebooks.com

The ship is slowly sinking.
I don't want to die in the icy black water.
When will help come?

TITANIC
The Story of a Disaster

In April 1912, the largest ship the world had ever seen set sail on her first voyage.

She was sailing from England to America.

Some passengers were taking a luxury holiday.

Others were travelling to a new life in America.

The ship was named

TITANIC...

...and she would never
reach America.

I am so cold.
So cold and scared.
I hear men shouting.
Women are crying.
I look over the railing into the
black water.
The ship is slowly sinking.

I don't want to die.
I don't want to die in the icy,
black water.

I am so cold.
So cold and scared.
The ship is slowly sinking.
When will help come?
I need to find my brother.

Where are you, Edward?
Please come and take care of me.

Mother died when I was a child.
So Edward took care of me.

When father beat me, Edward
wiped away my tears.

I was never scared if Edward
was there.

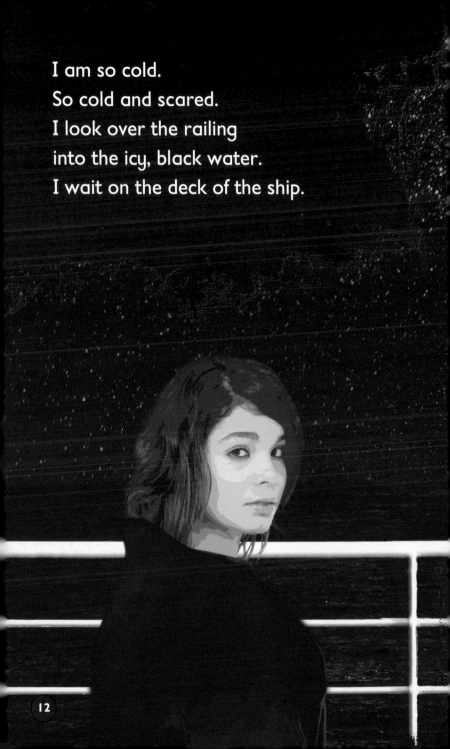

I am so cold.
So cold and scared.
I look over the railing
into the icy, black water.
I wait on the deck of the ship.

Where are you, Edward?
Please come and take care of me.

When I was 16, I fell in love.
He was a gardener at the
big house.

I knew what we did was wrong.
But then it was too late.

I was so scared.
I knew father would beat
me when he found out.
Edward wiped away my tears.
He said, "I will take care of you, Maggie."

I worked as a maid at the big house.
The mistress was young and kind.
She said, "We are going to visit
America, Maggie."

"We are going on a new ship."
"I want you to come with us."

I didn't know what to do.
My dress was growing tighter.
Father would beat me.

Edward said, "I will come with you
to America."
"I'll get work on the ship."
"I will take care of you, Maggie.
You and your baby."

Titanic was the most beautiful place
I'd ever seen.
My cabin was bigger than our whole cottage.
I helped the mistress unpack
her silk dresses.

My own dress was growing tighter.
But soon we would be in America.
Edward would take care of me
and my baby.

I went to Southampton with Maggie.
Titanic was the biggest ship I'd ever seen.
I waited on the dock.
Some lads had not shown up to work.

A man asked me, "Are you a stoker?"
I didn't know what a stoker did,
but I said yes!

The ship's boiler room was hot and dark.
It was in the deepest part of the ship.
It was the most hellish place I'd ever seen.
Hour after hour, I worked.
Shovelling coal to keep the boilers burning.

But soon we would be in America.
I would take care of Maggie.
Maggie and her baby.

It was my fifth night on the ship.
Suddenly I woke up.
I didn't know why.
The engines had stopped.
The mistress came into my cabin.

"Something bad has happened," she said.
"I want you to come with me."
"We must go up on deck."

I was shovelling coal.
Suddenly it happened.
A terrible sound of grinding metal.
I could hear men shouting.
"Stop the engines!"
I knew something bad
had happened.

I am so cold.
So cold and scared.
I wait on the deck of the ship.
The mistress climbed into a lifeboat.
She said, "I want you to come with me, Maggie."

But I couldn't leave.
Not without my brother.

I am so scared.
All around me there is steam and smoke.
The lads are shouting.
They say the ship is sinking.
But we have to keep the boilers burning.
The boilers keep the pumps working.
Without the pumps, the ship will
sink even faster.

But I want to find my sister.
Where are you, Maggie?

They say we hit an iceberg.
The ship is sinking into the
icy black water.

Some people escaped in lifeboats.
But there were not enough boats
for everyone.
People scream as they fall
from the deck.

I hold on tight to a railing.
Edward will find me soon,
he has to.
Help will come soon, it has to.

They say Titanic hit an iceberg.
The iceberg tore a huge hole in her side.
We kept the boilers burning.
We kept the pumps working.
But it was not enough.
The ship is sinking.

The boiler room is filling with water.
There's no chance for us lads down here.

The icy, black water fills my nose and mouth.
I can't breathe.
But I know you will be safe, Maggie.
You will be safe in a lifeboat.
Make a good life in America, Maggie.
I'm sorry, Maggie.

I am so cold.
So cold and scared.
I'm sinking into the icy black water.
I don't want to die.
I don't want my baby to die.

Someone please help me.
Someone please help us all.

TITANIC

Behind the Story

The *RMS Titanic* left Southampton on 10th April 1912, bound for America. On board were more than 2,200 passengers and crew.

At 11.40 pm on 14th April, *Titanic* struck an iceberg in the Atlantic Ocean. The iceberg tore a 90-metre-long gash in the ship. The crew soon realised that their new ship, which the world believed was unsinkable, was taking on water and sinking fast.

The ship's lifeboats were launched, with women and children given priority. There were not enough lifeboats, however, to hold everyone. Also, many lifeboats rowed away from the sinking ship half empty. The people left behind knew they were doomed. The men working in the boiler and engine rooms deep below deck stayed at their posts. They knew they would have no chance to escape when the end came.

Titanic sank in just two hours 40 minutes. There was no time for other ships to come to her rescue. Just over 700 people in the lifeboats survived and were later rescued by a ship called the *Carpathia*. More than 1,500 people drowned in the icy Atlantic Ocean.

Titanic's passengers travelled in first, second or third class. Many first class passengers were wealthy Americans who had been touring Europe. Many of the third class, or steerage, passengers were extremely poor people from Ireland. Some had sold everything they owned to buy a ticket to a new life in America.

TITANIC – *What's next?*

FLASHBACK
ON YOUR OWN

Maggie and Edward tell their stories using flashbacks. Movies often use flashbacks as a way to explain how a character came to be in a place or situation. Write a story that uses flashbacks. Think about:

• Where is your main character in the present day?

• What is the character feeling?

• Use flashbacks to explain the character's situation and how he or she is feeling.

TWO SIDES TO EVERY STORY
WITH A PARTNER

Maggie and Edward both talk about the same event but from different viewpoints. With a partner choose an event to talk about. It could be a concert you both went to or something that happened in your town. Each write down five memories of the event. Then take turns to read out a sentence.

• How are your memories alike? How are they different?

Maggie and Edward are characters in a story. Their story, however, is based on what happened to hundreds of people the night the *Titanic* sank. Discuss with your group how the story makes you feel. Think about:

- What did it feel like to be trapped on the ship knowing you would drown?

- The *Titanic* disaster happened more than 100 years ago. Why do you think people today are still so interested in the story?

DISCOVERING TITANIC
ON YOUR OWN / WITH A PARTNER

In 1985, underwater archaeologist Dr. Robert Ballard discovered the wreck of the *Titanic*.

Go online to find out more about Dr. Ballard's expeditions and to see photos and videos of the wreck of the *Titanic*.

This photo shows the bow, or front, of the Titanic.

Titles in the
Yesterday's Voices
series

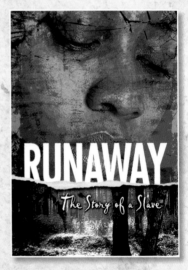

I waited deep below the arena.
Then it was my turn to fight.
Kill or be killed!

I cannot live as a slave
any longer. Tonight, I will
escape and never go back.

TITANIC
The Story of a Disaster

The ship is sinking into the icy sea. I don't want to die. Someone help us!

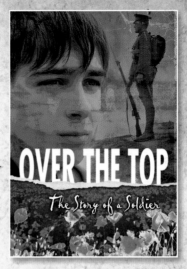

OVER THE TOP
The Story of a Soldier

I'm waiting in the trench. I am so afraid. Tomorrow we go over the top.

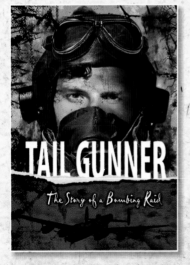

TAIL GUNNER
The Story of a Bombing Raid

Another night. Another bombing raid. Will this night be the one when we don't make it back?

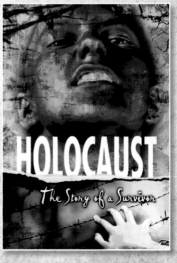

HOLOCAUST
The Story of a Survivor

They took my clothes and shaved my head. I was no longer a human.